HIPPO POTTO & MOUSE

Roger Hargreaves

P.S.I. & Associates, Inc.
13322 S.W. 128th Street
Miami, Florida 33186

If you come out of your house, turn left, and walk for nine hundred and ninety-nine miles, you will come to a house. Or rather a cottage. Christmas Cottage!

And in Christmas Cottage live those three very good friends—Hippo, Potto, and Mouse.
Hippo is a particularly earnest fellow. He goes to work every day in order to earn enough money so that he and Potto and Mouse can live very well.
Hippo worries a lot about money. In fact, he worries a lot about everything.

"Well, Mouse. What do you think?" called Potto over his shoulder. "Great," shouted Mouse at the top of his squeak as the wind whistled between his ears.

And on they flew. Potto and Mouse in their beautiful shiny bright red airplane.

Hippo was hard at work in his office.
"Time to go home soon," he thought, "and cook supper for Potto and Mouse."
He glanced out of his office window.
"Good Heavens," he gasped.
"Hello, Hippo," boomed Potto as he flew past the office window.
Hippo went white.

Poor Hippo grabbed his hat and ran out of his office and
all the way back to Christmas Cottage.
Potto had landed the airplane in the garden.
"Quite a surprise, don't you agree?"
he said, as Hippo came puffing up the garden path.

"But where did you get it?" sputtered Hippo.
"Bought it," replied Potto.
"But we can't possibly afford an
airplane," said Hippo.
"Nonsense," said Potto.
"But how much did it cost?"
asked Hippo.
"Oh, not very much," replied Potto,
"not very much at all. In fact, I didn't
even bother to ask!"
Hippo was
speechless.

Later that evening a discussion took place. "Why can't I keep it?" cried Potto for the hundredth time. "Oh, please let me keep it. Please please please please please please."

"No!" said Hippo.

"But," said Potto.

"No!" said Hippo.

"Please?" said Mouse.

"No!" said Hippo. "Tomorrow you will take it back!"

"But," said Potto.

"No!" said Hippo. "And that's final!"

The following day Hippo telephoned from his office. "Well, Potto," he said, "did you do it? Have you taken it back?"

"Yes," replied Potto grumpily. "Thank goodness," Hippo said, and put down the telephone. He heaved a sigh of relief and got on with his work.

That evening Hippo walked slowly home from work.
"Perhaps I have been a little hard on Potto," he thought
to himself. "But it really is for his own good!"
He walked wearily through the garden gate.
"Oh, no!" he gasped.
And what do you think he saw standing outside
Christmas Cottage?

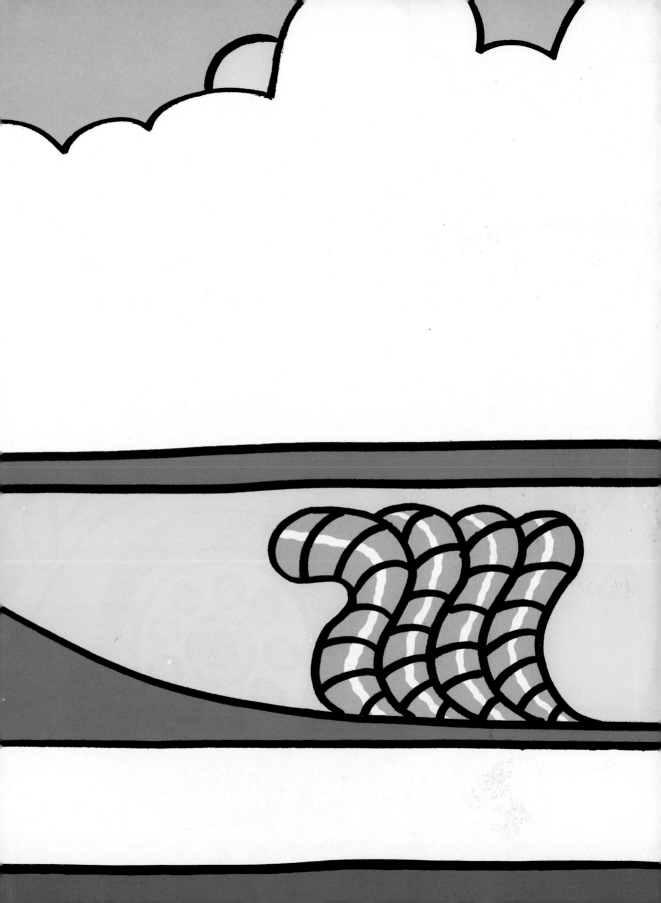

The longest, most
powerful, gleaming,
shining automobile.
"Hello, Hippo," shouted
Potto, sitting behind the
wheel of the car and
laughing. "Surprise.
Surprise!"
Oh, Potto!